FESTIVAL PICTURE READERS

my little Pony

Ponies know how to have fun! A game of hide-and-seek is the perfect pastime on a beautiful afternoon. But when Sparkleworks is nowhere to be found, the ponies decide to turn the tables and make *her* find *them*.

HarperFestival®
A Division of HarperCollins Publishers

Ages 3–6
© 2005 Hasbro, Inc. All rights reserved.
www.harperchildrens.com

my little Pony
1 point
Go to mylittlepony.com
for details!

Licensed by:

Hasbro
Properties
Group

US $3.99 / $5.99 CAN
ISBN 0-06-073270-9

73270

0 46594 00399 7

08-CXY-988

A NOTE TO PARENTS

Welcome to the world of Festival Readers!

These inviting, kids'-choice readers were created to help develop and nurture a love of reading that will last a lifetime. Festival Readers feature the characters that children love best; stories are told in brief, lively text and are complemented by illustrations to support every child's reading success.

We hope you and your child enjoy the pleasure this story brings, and that your child's world will be enriched by the adventure of reading. Here are a few tips you may find helpful:

- Find a comfortable setting in which to read together. You might create a "reading corner" in your child's room or any place that's quiet.
- Take your time, letting the story set the tone and pace.
- Follow the words with your fingers as you read, and give your child the job of turning the pages.
- As your child's reading skills improve, have him or her read the book to a younger sibling, a friend, or even a teddy bear.
- Be an enthusiastic audience and give lots of praise! Your words of encouragement play a crucial role in your child's confidence as a reader.

But where was Sparkleworks?

"We will help you find her!"

said Star Swirl.

Sweetberry found a .

Star Swirl found a little .

Petal Blossom found a .

But none of the ponies could

find Sparkleworks.

Can you?

"Sparkleworks is the best hider!" Meadowbrook whispered to the other three ponies. "If *we* can't find her, maybe we can make *her* find us. Let's have a party!"

Petal Blossom got

the .

Star Swirl gathered

pretty  in a bunch.

Sweetberry poured

make-believe .

Soon Sparkleworks heard

laughter in her .

She smelled the scent of

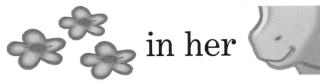 in her .

Then Sparkleworks'

peeked out.

She saw her friends

on the

having a fun party.

Sparkleworks came out of

her hiding place.

"Hiding is fun," she said.

"But finding your friends

is even better!"